A WALK TO THE GREAT MYSTERY

VIRGINIA A. STROUD

Dial Books for Young Readers *NEW YORK*

Published by Dial Books for Young Readers
A Division of Penguin Books USA Inc.
375 Hudson Street
New York, New York 10014
Copyright © 1995 by Virginia A. Stroud
Designed by Heather Wood
Printed in Hong Kong
First Edition
1 3 5 7 9 10 8 6 4 2

Library of Congress Cataloging in Publication Data
Stroud, Virginia A.
A walk to the Great Mystery / Virginia A. Stroud—1st ed.
p.   cm.
Summary: While exploring the woods with their grandmother, a Cherokee medicine woman,
two children learn about the spirit of life that is all around them and within them as well.
ISBN 0-8037-1636-2 (trade)—ISBN 0-8037-1637-0 (library)
1. Cherokee Indians—Juvenile fiction.   [1. Cherokee Indians—Fiction.
2. Indians of North America—Fiction. 3. Grandmothers—Fiction. 4. Nature—Fiction.]   I. Title.
PZ7.S9248Wal   1995   [E]—dc20   93-32340   CIP   AC

The artwork was prepared with acrylic paint, gouache paint, and ink on Museum Rag paper.
It was then color-separated and reproduced in full color.

To Max Luthy, for his words of encouragement
and his reminder that truth passes through three stages:

OPPOSITION • RIDICULE • SELF-EVIDENCE

ᴛHE MEDICINE HOOP shown on the jacket and in the last piece
of art is a symbol of transformation, of bringing the physical and spiritual worlds into
balance. It also represents new birth: Dustin and Rosie are being born into
the world of insight and the magic that is all around us. ∽ V. A. S.

The car bounced and swayed as it worked its way down the familiar, well-rutted gravel road. Sprinkles of wildflowers outlined the twisting lane, which eventually led over the wooden bridge that crossed Hesperus Creek.

The road went past the metal mailbox and its sign, "Fairy Ranch," to a

sun-washed gate. Beyond the gate was the small house trimmed in turquoise blue: Grandma Ann's house.

Grandma Ann was not like any other grown-up that Dustin and Rosie knew. She was a medicine woman, a healer, who had a special way of looking at life. "Some things you feel, and can't see; some things you see, and no one believes you," she liked to say.

Today Grandma Ann was already standing out on her covered porch, wiping her hands on a dish towel. Dustin and Rosie sprang from the car, swung open the gate, and ran straight into her open arms for one of her tight hugs. Their mother waved to Grandma Ann, and drove back down the bumpy road.

Inside Grandma Ann's house were all kinds of wonderful things: stacks of rocks, piles of seashells, baskets of feathers, deer antlers, mink tails, wishbones of hummingbirds. Always above her doorway hung an eagle's tail feather; Grandma Ann said that it kept bad energy from crossing the threshold.

Grandma Ann had already packed lunches, and she picked them up from the kitchen table. In her other hand she held a flour sack printed in red with the words "Blue Bird."

"Off we go," she announced. "We have a big day ahead of us."

"Where are we going, Grandma?" Rosie asked.

"To find the Great Mystery," she answered as she led them down the porch steps. "We'll start in the woods."

"What's the Great Mystery?" Dustin wanted to know.

"It's where the secrets of the earth come from," his grandmother answered.

"Have you been there, Grandma? Where is it?" Rosie asked excitedly.

"I've been there many times, and you'll see where it is," was all Grandma Ann would say.

"But why are we starting in the woods?" Dustin said.

Grandma Ann ruffled his hair. "If we were at your house, we'd start in the backyard. The woods are my backyard, so we'll begin here. Come on."

The house disappeared behind them as they walked into the woods.

"We will enter quietly," said Grandma Ann. "The rocks and trees, the leaves and the blades of grass—each has life, has a spirit. We will enter with much respect, trying not to disturb them."

Rosie and Dustin watched as she began to scan the ground in a sweeping motion, looking left to right, right to left. Rosie mimicked her grandmother. She knew Grandma would get to the Great Mystery, whatever it was, and she wanted to make sure she arrived at the same moment.

Grandma Ann stopped, bent down, and picked up an object. "This is for you, Rosie," she said. "What do you see?"

"A rock?" said Rosie, confused. "A black rock."

"Look again, Rosie. Look closely in the light," said Grandma Ann.

"It sparkles and glitters," Rosie said, turning the rock over in her hand.

"Yes, Rosie. The sparkling light will carry you to the Great Mystery."

"What about me?" interrupted Dustin. "Where's my rock? How do I get to the Great Mystery?"

Grandma Ann glanced at Dustin and smiled. A few steps later she bent down. "Here, Dustin, this stone is for you," she said as she brushed the loose dirt from the rock. "What do you see?" she asked, placing it in the boy's open palm.

"A gray rock…" Dustin studied it carefully. "With a line that goes around and around."

"Yes," said Grandma Ann, pointing. "Do you see it's like a spiral, circling from bottom to top like a bird circles up, up to the sky?" she asked. "It's taking you to flight and the Great Mystery."

"This old rock can do that?" asked Dustin.

Grandma Ann stopped in her tracks and turned to face the children. "Oh, yes! These rocks have worked their way from the center of the world, pushing and moving up to the back of Mother Earth. They have collected knowledge on their journey."

"Let's have lunch," Rosie suggested. "All this walking is making me hungry."

They walked on through the woods to the bank of the little stream, now just a trickle in the hot August sun. As the children sat down, Grandma Ann suddenly knelt near the water. "Would you look at that! A heart-shaped rock." She showed it to Dustin and Rosie. "See? The earth loves us so much, she gives us her heart." Grandma Ann carefully placed the stone in her flour sack and sat beside the children.

"What all do you carry in that sack?" Rosie asked.

"My medicine tools, treasures that I've collected on my walks," said Grandma Ann.

"Can we see?" asked Dustin.

Grandma hesitated. "These are tools that remind me of where all of life's powers come from," she explained. "I can show you some of the things I carry; some you are not ready for now."

She reached deep down inside the bag and pulled out a rock with a line that spiraled around and around it. Dustin beamed and looked at his own rock.

Next came a bundle of dried plants bound in red thread.

"Weeds?" asked Dustin.

"Sagebrush," Grandma Ann told him. Then she brought out a cellophane bag that made a clinking sound.

"Pennies!" exclaimed Rosie.

"Yes, made of copper," answered Grandma Ann. "I will use the copper and sagebrush later, when the day is over, for a blessing."

Then came a tiny feather. Grandma Ann held it between her fingers. "Hummingbird's tail feather," she remarked.

"Is there anything else you can show us, Grandma?" Rosie wanted to know.

"Oh, I almost forgot! I have something for you," Grandma Ann exclaimed, handing Dustin and Rosie each a folded bundle. Grins appeared on the children's faces as they unfolded the material and read the words "Blue Bird." Dustin and Rosie immediately dropped their rocks into their medicine tool sacks.

After they had eaten their sandwiches, Grandma Ann stood up. "Want to learn more?"

"Yes," the children chimed in together. "But, Grandma, what about the Great Mystery?" Dustin asked.

"You'll see," said Grandma Ann. "Now, tell me what you know about trees. What does a tree give you?"

"Flowers, fruit, houses for the birds," Dustin guessed.

"Firewood, paper, and shade," said Rosie.

"What else?" asked Grandma Ann. The children looked at each other, trying to find another answer, but with no luck.

"Smells?" their grandmother finally suggested.

"Oh, yeah," said Rosie. "The smell of leaves and bark."

Dustin picked up a branch and sniffed the wood. "It smells like dust to me," he said.

"Come here," said Grandma Ann as she led the children to a ponderosa pine. The three of them stood at the base of the tree trunk. Grandma Ann reached out and patted the pine tree. "Hello," she said softly. She lifted her chin ever so slightly and pressed it to a crack in the trunk. "I've brought my grandchildren to meet you. Come closer, children. Place your hand on the tree. Give it a hug and let it feel you back. Now say hello and ask if you can smell its center."

Rosie placed her nose close to the tree. "I'm Rosie. Can I smell your center?" she asked, then jerked back, rubbing her nose and giggling. "Dustin, it smells just like vanilla! Try it," she said.

Dustin approached the tree and gave it a hug. "Hello, I'm Dustin. Can I smell your center too?" He pressed his nose against the pine and took a deep breath. He pulled back slowly and looked high up in its branches. "Vanilla," he whispered. "Do they all smell like that, Grandma?"

"Well," answered Grandma Ann, "some will smell like chocolate or cherry. They are different, just like all of us are different. Now," she said, looking around. "We'll head over there, where the boulders live, next. But first, can you stand still and listen?"

The children did, and they heard the birds sing and the frogs call for rain.

A hummingbird buzzed past Dustin's ear. He brushed it away, but his grandmother said, "Stop, Dustin! The hummingbird is blessing you with joy and happiness. Pretend to be a statue; let him look in your eyes."

Dustin held very still, hardly daring to breathe, as the hummingbird hovered near his face. Then it zipped on.

"He recognized your inner light," Grandma Ann explained. "The light that glows inside you that our eyes can't see."

"Grandma Ann, look at all the white butterflies!" Rosie cried. "They're really flying. Do they have a message too?"

"Oh, yes. When a butterfly comes to you, especially a white one, it carries a question about your life. It asks you to look at any problem you might have to see what stage you're in. There are four: egg, the beginning; caterpillar stage, when you should move ahead, but slowly; cocoon, time to sit on things awhile; and butterfly stage—time to spread your wings and fly with your ideas."

Dustin and Rosie looked at each other and smiled, taking Grandma Ann's outstretched hands as they walked quietly through the woods. All three dangled their flour sacks.

When they reached the place where several boulders jutted out from the earth, Grandma Ann stopped and began to climb the largest boulder. She motioned for the children to follow. "Mind your steps," she ordered.

After they were settled, she instructed them to lie back with their shoulders flat against the boulder. "What do you feel, Rosie?" she asked, watching them.

"A tingling on my back."

Dustin observed, "I feel like I could sink into the rock."

"Yes," said Grandma Ann, "we'll go into the boulder. Ready? Hold my hands."

The children weren't sure exactly how long they lay on the boulder, holding their grandmother's hands. But after some time both of them saw the light around them begin to grow dark. They could still hear the forest sounds, could still see the tree branches and sky, yet they seemed to be melting into the boulder. Its granite seemed to surround them as deeper and deeper they sank. Then suddenly, as easily as they had entered the boulder, they were released from its hold. Rosie and Dustin sat up beside their grandmother and looked at each other in surprise.

"Was that the Great Mystery, Grandma?" Rosie asked as they headed back toward the path.

"Part of it, Rosie. What do you suppose the Great Mystery is? What did the rocks, the trees, the hummingbird, the white butterflies, and the boulder show you?" Grandma Ann sat down to wait for her grandchildren's answers. She patted the ground and they sat too.

"Life?" said Dustin.

"Yes, very good. It's the spirit of all living things, and it shows its secrets only when we pay attention," Grandma Ann said, smiling.

"Then," began Rosie, "the Great Mystery is all around us every day?"

"Inside us too," said Dustin. "Right? Like when the hummingbird came and looked in my eyes?"

"Oh, you two are such good students," Grandma Ann said and gave them another of her warm hugs.

Then she reached for her flour sack. "You children go on back toward the house. I would like to give thanks now alone for this special day. I'll catch up soon."

As Dustin and Rosie carried their cotton sacks up the dark path through the woods, a white butterfly fluttered ahead, leading them to the brilliant light of day and Grandma Ann's house.